VRITRA:

The guardian of dharma

by

Kiran Khugsal Upreti

DEDICATION

To the unwavering protectors of light, both seen and unseen, who stand against the darkness with courage, wisdom, and compassion. This tale is for those who believe in the power of love, duty, and the strength of the human spirit.

ACKNOWLEDGEMENT

Writing *Vritra: The Guardian of Dharma* has been an incredible journey, and I owe a deep sense of gratitude to the people who have supported and inspired me along the way.

First and foremost, I dedicate this work to the Divine. Your guidance and blessings have been the light that illuminated my path, allowing me to bring this story to life.

I want to express my heartfelt thanks to my husband, Dr. Kartikeya Upreti. Your unwavering support, insightful conversations, and belief in my vision have been the cornerstone of this work. Thank you for being my partner in every sense of the word.

To my mother-in-law, Prof. Jaya Upreti, your wisdom and encouragement have been invaluable. Your scholarly insights and understanding of the deeper aspects of Vedic knowledge have enriched this novel in more ways than I can express.

I am deeply grateful to my parents, Ramesh Chandra Khugsal and Harshi Khugsal, whose love and values have shaped who I am today. Your unwavering belief in me has been my strength, and I dedicate this work to you both.

To my brother, Anshul Khugsal, and my sister, Jyoti Khugsal, thank you for your constant support and for always being there to cheer me on. Your encouragement has meant the world to me.

Finally, I extend my deepest appreciation to all my readers. Thank you for embarking on this journey with Vritra and for believing in the power of stories to illuminate the path of dharma.

Table of Contents

PAGE NO

Chapter 1: *The Prophecy Fulfilled*

In the tranquil village of Devpur, life moved at a gentle pace, guided by the rhythms of the Ganges River and the teachings of ancient Vedic traditions. It was a place where the people lived in harmony with nature, their lives intertwined with rituals that honored the gods and revered the knowledge passed down through generations. Among the villagers, Raghunath and Sumitra stood out as a couple of great wisdom and virtue, respected by all. They had longed for a child for many years, and when Sumitra finally became pregnant, it was seen as a blessing from the gods.

One fateful night, as the village lay wrapped in the quiet embrace of sleep, Sumitra went into labor. The skies above Devpur were unusually clear, with the stars shining brighter than ever before. As Raghav entered the world, a strange phenomenon occurred: the wind ceased to blow, the animals in the village became silent, and the waters of the Ganges seemed to glow with a soft, ethereal light. It was as if the entire world was holding its breath, awaiting the arrival of someone extraordinary.

The village priest, a venerable sage named Rishi Agastya, arrived at Raghunath and Sumitra's home shortly after the birth. His keen senses had detected a powerful energy, unlike anything he had felt before. Upon seeing the newborn, Rishi Agastya's eyes widened with recognition. He had spent decades studying the ancient texts and prophecies, and he knew that the child before him was no ordinary infant.

"This boy," he whispered, more to himself than to the parents, "is the one spoken of in the prophecies. He carries within him the essence of the ancient gods. He is the rebirth of Vritra, but this time, he is destined to protect, not to destroy."

Raghunath and Sumitra listened with growing awe as Rishi Agastya explained the significance of their son's birth. According to the scriptures, Vritra had once been a mighty asura (rakshasa) who had challenged the gods, particularly Indra, the king of the heavens. After a fierce battle, Vritra was defeated by Indra's weapon, the Vajra, and was subsequently cursed to be reborn as a guardian of dharma – a being who would protect the balance between good and evil.

However, Raghav was not merely a reincarnation of Vritra; he was something more. He was destined to inherit the powers of the gods, but these powers would only be unlocked when he reached the age of 23 – the age at which he would possess the wisdom, knowledge, and discernment necessary to wield them responsibly.

Rishi Agastya placed his hand on the child's forehead and uttered a series of ancient mantras, invoking the blessings of the divine. As he did so, a faint golden light enveloped Raghav, a sign that the gods had acknowledged the child's destiny. "You must raise him with great care," the priest advised Raghunath and Sumitra. "Teach him the ways of dharma, instill in him a sense of justice, and prepare him for the great responsibility that lies ahead. When the time comes, he will be ready to fulfill his purpose."

As Raghav grew, it became clear that he was no ordinary child. From a young age, he exhibited an extraordinary intellect and a natural affinity for learning. He absorbed the teachings of the Vedas, Upanishads, and Puranas with ease, often surprising the village elders with his profound understanding of complex spiritual concepts. His memory was exceptional, allowing him to recite long passages of scripture without error.

Rishi Agastya took a special interest in Raghav's education, recognizing that the boy was destined for greatness. Under the priest's guidance, Raghav was trained in the art of meditation, yoga, and the chanting of ancient shlokas. Each day, he would rise before dawn to perform his rituals, offering prayers to the gods and seeking their guidance. The villagers often remarked that Raghav seemed to possess an inner calm and focus that belied his age, as if he were already in communion with higher powers.

As part of his training, Raghav was also taught the importance of discipline and self-control. Rishi Agastya emphasized that true power could only be wielded by those who had mastered themselves. "Your mind is your greatest weapon," the priest would often say. "Learn to control it, and you will control the world around you."

Raghav's days were filled with rigorous study and practice, but he never complained. He understood that his life had a purpose far greater than his own desires. The teachings of dharma were deeply ingrained in him, guiding his every thought and action. He was taught to discern right from wrong, to act with compassion, and to uphold the principles of justice in all that he did.

Despite his extraordinary abilities, Raghav was humble and kind, never seeking to elevate himself above others. He was well-liked by the villagers, who saw in him a young man of great promise. They often sought his advice on matters of spiritual and moral significance, and Raghav would offer his insights with the wisdom of someone far beyond his years.

When Raghav turned 18, Rishi Agastya deemed him ready to learn the truth about his destiny. He took the young man to a secluded part of the village, where an ancient temple dedicated to the gods stood. The temple had long been abandoned, its once-grand walls now covered in vines and moss. Inside, however, the air was thick with divine energy, a remnant of the powerful rituals that had been performed there centuries ago.

"Raghav," Rishi Agastya began, "the time has come for you to learn about the power that resides within you. You are the reincarnation of Vritra, but unlike your previous life, you have been chosen by the gods to protect the world from the forces of darkness. The powers you will inherit are not of this world; they are gifts from the gods themselves, bestowed upon you to fulfill your destiny."

The priest led Raghav to a hidden chamber within the temple, where three ancient weapons lay on a stone altar. The weapons – a trident (Trishula), a discus (Sudarshana Chakra), and a bow (Dhanush) – were no ordinary artifacts; they were imbued with the power of the gods.

"These are the weapons of Shiva, Vishnu, and Rama," Rishi Agastya explained. "Each of these weapons holds immense power, but they can only be wielded by one who is pure of heart and strong of mind. When you reach the age of 23, the power of these weapons will awaken within you, and you will be able to summon them at will. Until then, you must continue your training, for the responsibility that comes with this power is great."

Raghav listened with rapt attention, understanding the gravity of what was being revealed to him. The Trishula represented the power of destruction and regeneration, the Sudarshana Chakra symbolized divine justice, and the Dhanush was the embodiment of righteous warfare. Each weapon was a manifestation of a specific aspect of dharma, and it would be Raghav's duty to wield them in the service of the gods.

Years passed, and Raghav's 23rd birthday approached. As the day drew nearer, he began to experience strange visions during his meditations – images of a vast mountain range, a hidden cave, and a voice calling out to him from the depths of the earth. It was the same voice he had heard in his childhood, but now it was more urgent, more insistent.

Raghav knew that the time had come for him to fulfill his destiny. He approached Rishi Agastya for guidance, and the priest confirmed his suspicions. "The Himalayas are calling you," he said. "There, you will find the source of your power – the fragment of the Vajra, the thunderbolt weapon of Indra. This is the final piece of the puzzle, the last step in your journey to becoming Vritra, the protector of dharma. Go, Raghav, and may the gods be with you."

With the blessings of his parents and the villagers, Raghav set out on his journey to the Himalayas. The path was treacherous, filled with rocky terrain, freezing temperatures, and the ever-present danger of avalanches. But Raghav pressed on, driven by an unshakable sense of purpose.

After days of arduous travel, he finally arrived at the mouth of a massive cave, just as he had seen in his visions. The entrance was adorned with ancient Sanskrit inscriptions and intricate murals that seemed to pulse with otherworldly energy. Taking a deep breath, Raghav stepped inside, knowing that his life was about to change forever. As he ventured deeper into the cave, the voice that had guided him all these years grew louder, clearer.

Chapter 2: *The Touch of Divine Power*

Raghav's heart pounded as he followed the mysterious voice echoing through the Himalayan caves. The ancient power that had been calling to him for months now felt tantalizingly close. With each step, the air grew thinner, and the path more treacherous, but Raghav pressed on, driven by an insatiable curiosity and a sense of destiny.

As he rounded a sharp bend, Raghav suddenly found himself face to face with a massive cavern entrance. Ancient Sanskrit inscriptions and intricate murals adorned its walls, pulsing with an otherworldly energy. Taking a deep breath, he stepped inside.

The cave's interior was bathed in an eerie blue light emanating from a small object at its center. Raghav's eyes widened as he recognized it – a fragment of the legendary Vajra, the thunderbolt weapon of the gods. As if in a trance, he reached out to touch it.

The moment his fingers brushed the Vajra's surface, a jolt of electricity surged through his body. Raghav gasped, his vision blurring as images of ancient battles and cosmic powers flashed before his eyes. He felt as if he was being torn apart and remade, molecule by molecule.

Suddenly, a bone-chilling roar shattered the silence. From the shadows emerged a monstrous figure – a rakshasa of legend, its eyes glowing with malevolence. "Who dares to touch the power of the gods?" it snarled, baring razor-sharp fangs.

Raghav stumbled backward, his heart racing. But as the rakshasa lunged forward, something extraordinary happened. The Vajra fragment in Raghav's hand pulsed with blinding light, and instinctively, he raised it as a shield.

To his amazement, an impenetrable barrier of energy formed around him, deflecting the rakshasa's attack. Raghav felt power coursing through his veins, ancient knowledge flooding his mind. Without knowing how, he began chanting in a language he had never spoken before.

The rakshasa howled in fury, unleashing a barrage of dark magic. But with each attack, Raghav grew stronger, more confident. He wasn't just defending anymore; he was fighting back.

As the battle raged on, Raghav felt himself changing. His body became infused with divine energy, his senses sharpened to superhuman levels. He was no longer just a village boy – he was becoming something more, something ancient and powerful.

In a desperate move, the rakshasa summoned a massive bolt of dark lightning, hurling it at Raghav with all its might. But in that crucial moment, Raghav's instincts took over. He caught the bolt with his bare hands, feeling its immense power coursing through him.

With a primal yell, Raghav redirected the rakshasa's own attack back at it. The cave exploded with light and sound as the dark creature was struck by its own power. When the dust settled, the rakshasa was gone, leaving only scorch marks on the cave floor.

Panting heavily, Raghav looked down at his hands in disbelief. They crackled with residual energy, and he could feel the power of the Vajra now pulsing in harmony with his own heartbeat. He had not just survived the encounter – he had been transformed by it.

As the adrenaline faded, questions flooded Raghav's mind. What had he become? What was the extent of his new powers? And most importantly, what was he meant to do with them?

Determined to find answers, Raghav began exploring the cave, studying the ancient inscriptions and artifacts with newfound understanding. Hours turned into days as he immersed himself in forgotten knowledge, slowly piecing together the puzzle of his destiny.

Finally, emerging from the cave, Raghav looked towards his village in the distance. He was no longer the same person who had left it. He was Vritra now – guardian of ancient powers and protector of dharma. With this realization came a sense of purpose and responsibility that both exhilarated and terrified him.

As the sun set over the Himalayas, casting long shadows across the valley, Vritra made a solemn vow. He would master these new abilities and use them to defend the world against the dark forces that lurked in the shadows. His journey as a guardian had only just begun, and the greatest challenges still lay ahead.

Little did Vritra know that his transformation had not gone unnoticed. In the ethereal realm of the gods, ancient eyes had watched his battle with keen interest. And in the darkest corners of the world, malevolent forces stirred, sensing the emergence of a new power that threatened their dominion. The stage was set for a cosmic conflict that would shape the fate of the world.

Chapter 3: *The Unveiling of Powers*

Vritra's journey into the world of his newfound powers was not an easy one. Every step he took was filled with caution and awe as he slowly began to understand and test the abilities that now resided within him. One day, while exploring the dense forests that bordered his village, he discovered something extraordinary. With a mere gesture, he summoned flames from thin air, manipulating the fire as though it were an extension of his own will. The flames danced at his fingertips, obeying his every command as he weaved them into complex patterns.

As days turned into weeks, Vritra's control over fire grew more precise and powerful. Yet, his abilities didn't stop there. One fateful afternoon, a fierce storm rolled in, and with it came a massive bolt of lightning. Without hesitation, Vritra reached out, and to his amazement, he caught the lightning in his hands. The raw, untamed energy crackled within his grasp, yet he felt no pain. Instead, he realized that he could channel this energy, turning it into a weapon of immense destruction or a shield of impenetrable defense.

The realization of his abilities filled Vritra with a sense of purpose, but also with the weight of responsibility. Unsure of how to proceed, he sought the counsel of his wise and revered guru, the village priest. When Vritra shared his experiences, the priest listened with deep concern, but also with understanding.

"These powers are a gift, Vritra, but they are also a test. You must learn to control them, to understand their true nature, and most importantly, to use them for the greater good," the priest advised.

With this guidance, the priest introduced Vritra to the ancient scriptures, the Vedas, and the sacred knowledge contained within them. Immersed in these teachings, Vritra's understanding of his powers deepened. He learned to chant mantras that could summon the elements, control the forces of nature, and even fortify his body against any harm. The priest also began to train him in the art of ancient weapons, teaching him to wield the divine arms of the gods with skill and precision.

Soon, Vritra was no longer the ordinary youth his village once knew. His body emanated a powerful aura, and his eyes gleamed with an otherworldly light. The villagers, noticing the transformation, whispered among themselves, both in awe and fear.

One day, while walking through the village, Vritra noticed people pointing at him, their eyes wide with curiosity and apprehension. He realized that his growing powers were becoming too apparent. The time had come to conceal his true identity.

Vritra hurried home, where his parents, Raghunath and Sumitra, were waiting for him. They were stunned by the change in their son's appearance. "What has happened to you, my son? You look so different, so... powerful," his father asked, his voice a mix of pride and worry.

Vritra took a deep breath and revealed everything to his parents—the powers, the training, and the realization of his destiny. "Mother, Father, I have been chosen as the protector of these ancient powers. My duty is to guard this world against the darkness that threatens it."

Raghunath and Sumitra listened, their hearts heavy with concern. "We are proud of you, my son, but we fear for your safety. How will you protect yourself?" Sumitra asked, her voice trembling.

Vritra smiled, a serene confidence in his eyes. "I have been given these powers for a reason, and I will use them wisely. I will remain hidden in the village, and when the time comes, I will rise to face the evil that threatens us all."

His parents, though anxious, could see the determination in Vritra's eyes. They blessed him, saying, "We will support you in your mission. May the gods protect you and guide you as you fulfill your destiny."

With his parents' blessings, Vritra knew that his journey had only just begun. He returned to the village, aware that greater challenges awaited him. The battles ahead would test not only his strength but also his resolve. But Vritra was ready, for he had embraced his destiny as the guardian of ancient powers, the protector of light in a world teetering on the edge of darkness.

Chapter 4: *Aghoraghata' s havoc*

In a distant town, chaos began to unfold without warning. People were acting erratically—some were gripped by inexplicable fear, while others succumbed to madness, behaving violently or even harming themselves. The authorities were baffled, unable to comprehend the cause of this bizarre behavior.

When news of this reached the village by the banks of the Ganges, Raghav, who was now fully embracing his identity as Vritra, felt a deep unease. He sensed that a dark and ancient power was behind these disturbing events. Seeking guidance, he went to his guru, the village priest.

The priest's face grew grim. "My son," he said, "this is the work of an ancient rakshasa. Its goal is to sow chaos and destroy the very fabric of righteousness and justice. This is the evil force you were destined to confront."

Raghav's heart raced with apprehension. "Guruji, how can I face this rakshasa? I've only tested my powers in your presence. What if it's stronger than I am?"

The priest's eyes gleamed with confidence. "You are Vritra, the protector. Within you lies the boundless power of Vedic knowledge and ancient mantras. But remember, true strength comes not just from power but from wisdom and courage. The time has come. Go, face your enemy."

With his guru's blessings, Raghav set out for the troubled town, fully aware of the monumental challenge that awaited him. The rakshasa's whereabouts were unknown, but Raghav was determined to track it down.

Upon reaching the town, Raghav immediately began investigating the strange occurrences. He observed that people were under the influence of an invisible force—some were delirious, while others lay unconscious. He was now certain that this was the work of rakshasa.

Reaching out to his guru once more, Raghav followed his instructions and embarked on a quest to find the rakshasa. He learned that this formidable entity was known as Aghoraghata, a powerful being using ancient Vedic spells and weapons to dominate and control the minds of the townsfolk.

Sensing that someone had come to challenge him, Aghoraghata unleashed his full might. The sky darkened as a thick, malevolent cloud spread across the horizon, bringing with it a foul stench and a fierce wind that sent the town into further panic.

Aghoraghata, channeling his malevolent energy, began to take on terrifying forms, wreaking havoc in the town.

He transformed into a monstrous figure, crushing everything in his path. He was using its supernatural abilities to hurl objects through the air and control the minds of terrified citizens. Recognizing Aghoraghata as the one he had heard about, Vritra steeled himself and advanced.

Aghoraghata noticed him and, with a cruel laugh, sneered, "Ah, another toy has come to join my game." Vritra stood firm. "Your reign of terror ends here, vile Aghoraghata. I will defeat you and free this city from your grip."

The Aghoraghata unleashed a surge of dark energy towards Vritra, but he swiftly raised his Vajra and countered the attack. When Vritra finally confronted him, he was taken aback by its sheer power. Aghoraghata was indeed more powerful than he had anticipated. But despite the fear gripping his heart, Vritra stood his ground, determined to face Aghorghata. Thus began a fierce and relentless battle between the two.

Drawing on his mantras, Vritra summoned all his powers, launching waves of fire, gusts of wind, and chanting ancient mantras, but Aghoraghata was formidable, parrying each of his attacks with ease. The city trembled as their battle raged on, and the townspeople, paralyzed with fear, took refuge wherever they could.

Some brave souls attempted to aid Vritra, but the fierce Aghoraghata easily overpowered them, bending their wills to his own. The struggle between Vritra and Aghoraghata grew more intense with each passing moment, and despite his valiant efforts, Vritra found himself increasingly worn down by Aghorghata's relentless onslaught.

Finally, Aghorghata delivered a devastating blow, leaving Vritra weakened and forcing him to retreat. He loomed over him, preparing to deliver the final strike. But in that critical moment, Vritra summoned every ounce of his strength. With one final, mighty effort, he unleashed a thunderous strike with his Vajra, shattering Aghotghata's power and sending it fleeing in defeat.

Exhausted and battered, Vritra had emerged victorious.Peace returned to the city, and the people hailed Vritra as a hero, praising his bravery and valor. However, Vritra knew that this was only the beginning of his journey. He realized that he needed to further develop his powers to face the rakshasa again, and the other dark forces that awaited him.

Chapter 5: *The rise of hidden enemy*

Vritra's victory over the rakshasa had brought a temporary calm to the village, a much-needed respite after the chaos that had gripped the city. The people of the village hailed him as a hero, and life began to return to normal. But unknown to them, a new danger was lurking in the shadows.

One day, a stranger arrived in the village. His name was Sudhir, a man of humble appearance and gentle demeanor. He quickly made himself useful, helping the villagers with their daily tasks, helping wherever needed, and gradually winning their trust. His smile was warm, his words kind, and soon enough, he became a beloved member of the community.

Sudhir's intentions, however, were far from noble. Beneath his amiable exterior, he was a cunning spy sent by the very rakshasa Vritra had defeated. The rakshasa, though temporarily vanquished, had not been destroyed. It had retreated, licking its wounds, and plotting its revenge. Sudhir was its agent, tasked with learning Vritra's secrets and exploiting his weaknesses.

Sudhir's first task was to gain Vritra's trust, and he did so with a calculated charm. He offered his help in the village, where Vritra often worked to rebuild what had been destroyed during the previous battle. He listened intently whenever Vritra spoke, pretending to be in awe of the hero's strength and wisdom. Slowly but surely, he ingratiated himself with Vritra, becoming a close companion.

Vritra, for his part, saw nothing suspicious in Sudhir's behavior. The battle with the rakshasa had left him weary, and he was grateful for the company of someone who seemed genuinely interested in helping the village recover. He welcomed Sudhir's friendship, sharing stories of his past battles and the challenges he faced. Vritra even began to confide in Sudhir, discussing his fears and doubts.

As their friendship grew, Sudhir started to subtly probe Vritra about his powers. He asked seemingly innocent questions about the source of Vritra's strength, how he had learned to control his abilities, and what his greatest vulnerabilities were. Vritra, believing Sudhir to be a loyal friend, answered these questions without hesitation. He spoke of the ancient mantras he had mastered, the rituals that gave him strength, and the few moments of doubt that had almost led to his downfall.

Sudhir listened carefully, storing away every detail. He was a patient man, and he knew that the time to strike would come soon. He continued to play the role of the faithful friend, all the while feeding information back to his master, the rakshasa, who was slowly regaining its strength.

Then came the day when Sudhir decided to put his plan into action. He suggested to Vritra that they take a walk in the forest, a place where they could speak without interruption. Vritra agreed, seeing no reason to suspect his friend. The two men set off together, chatting amiably as they ventured deeper into the woods.

As they walked, Sudhir began to subtly steer the conversation toward Vritra's recent battle with the rakshasa. He asked about the strategies Vritra had used, the moments when he had felt most vulnerable. Vritra, still unsuspecting, answered truthfully, recounting the fierce struggle and the moments when he had doubted whether he would prevail.

Sudhir listened intently, his mind working quickly. He had learned enough. Without warning, he attacked.

Vritra was caught completely off guard. Sudhir, who had always seemed so mild and gentle, suddenly transformed before his eyes. His friendly face twisted into a sneer, and his body began to change. His muscles bulged, his skin darkened, and a terrible, otherworldly energy radiated from him. Sudhir revealed his true form—a powerful rakshasa, sent by Vritra's old enemy to destroy him.

Vritra barely had time to react before Sudhir struck, launching a powerful blow that sent him crashing to the ground. He struggled to his feet, trying to comprehend what had just happened. How could he have been so blind? How could he have trusted this monster?

But there was no time for self-recrimination. Sudhir was upon him again, his attacks relentless. Vritra fought back, but he was at a disadvantage. Sudhir had learned his weaknesses, and he exploited them mercilessly. Every time Vritra tried to summon his powers, Sudhir countered with a dark spell or a physical attack that left him reeling.

The forest around them seemed to pulse with the energy of their battle. Trees cracked and splintered under the force of their blows, the ground trembled, and the air was thick with the scent of magic. Vritra realized that this was unlike any battle he had fought before. Sudhir was not just a powerful opponent—he was someone who knew Vritra's innermost thoughts and fears, someone who had used his trust against him.

As the fight raged on, Vritra found himself weakening. Sudhir's attacks were relentless, and Vritra's strength was waning. He tried to remember the teachings of his guru, the mantras that had given him power in his previous battles, but his mind was clouded with doubt and confusion. He had trusted Sudhir, and that trust had been betrayed. How could he fight someone who had been his friend?

Sudhir sensed Vritra's hesitation and pressed his advantage. He unleashed a barrage of dark energy that sent Vritra crashing to the ground once more. This time, Vritra struggled to rise. His body was battered, his energy nearly spent. Sudhir loomed over him, a triumphant smile on his twisted face.

"Did you really think you could defeat me, Vritra?" Sudhir sneered. "Did you really think you could trust anyone? You're a fool, and now you'll pay the price for your stupidity."

Vritra felt a wave of despair wash over him. Sudhir was right—he had been foolish to trust so easily, to let his guard down. But as he lay there, beaten and broken, something stirred within him. A memory of his guru's teachings, of the strength that came not just from power, but from resolve and determination.

With a supreme effort, Vritra forced himself to stand. He drew on the last reserves of his strength, focusing his mind on the one thing that had always given him power—his purpose. He was not fighting for himself, but for the village, for the people who depended on him. He could not let them down.

Sudhir saw Vritra rise and laughed. "Still standing, are you? It won't matter. You're finished, Vritra."

But Vritra was no longer listening. He closed his eyes, muttering the ancient mantras under his breath. He felt the energy surge within him, the power that came from his connection to the divine. The ground beneath him trembled, and the air around him crackled with energy.

Sudhir's smile faltered as he sensed the shift in Vritra's aura. He lunged forward, hoping to finish the fight before Vritra could regain his full strength, but it was too late. Vritra's eyes snapped open, glowing with a fierce light. He raised his hand, and a beam of pure, radiant energy shot out, striking Sudhir square in the chest.

The force of the blast sent Sudhir flying backward. He crashed into a tree with a sickening thud, his body smoking from the impact. Vritra didn't wait for him to recover. He advanced quickly, summoning another surge of energy and launching it at the fallen rakshasa.

Sudhir screamed in agony as the energy engulfed him. His form flickered and twisted, the rakshasa's true nature struggling to maintain its hold on the physical world. Vritra continued to press the attack, pouring all his remaining strength into the assault. He knew this was his only chance to end the fight, to defeat the hidden enemy who had betrayed him.

Sudhir's body convulsed as the energy tore through him. His human disguise melted away, revealing the monstrous creature beneath. The rakshasa's skin cracked and blistered, its eyes burning with fury and pain. It tried to retaliate, to summon one last burst of dark power, but Vritra's attack was too strong. The rakshasa's form began to disintegrate, its essence unraveling in the face of Vritra's divine might.

With a final, ear-piercing scream, Sudhir was consumed by the light. His body disintegrated into ash, and the dark energy that had surrounded him dissipated into the air. The forest fell silent, the only sound the ragged breathing of Vritra as he stood over the spot where his enemy had been.

Vritra's victory was hard-won, but it came at a cost. He was exhausted, his body battered and bruised. But more than that, he was shaken by the realization that he had been so easily deceived. He had trusted Sudhir, had allowed himself to believe in the goodness of a stranger, and that trust had nearly led to his downfall.

As he slowly made his way back to the village, Vritra reflected on the lesson he had learned. The world was full of dangers, not all of them as obvious as a rakshasa in battle. Some enemies hid behind friendly smiles and kind words, waiting for the right moment to strike. Vritra knew he would have to be more vigilant in the future, to guard not just his body, but his heart as well.

When Vritra returned to the village, the people greeted him with cheers and praise. They had heard the sounds of the battle in the forest and knew that their hero had once again defended them from a great evil. But Vritra could not share in their joy. The memory of Sudhir's betrayal weighed heavily on him, a reminder that even the greatest warriors could be brought low by deceit.

Vritra sat alone by the river that ran through the village, his thoughts troubled. The moonlight reflected off the water, casting a pale glow over his weary form. The weight of the battle, both physical and emotional, pressed down on him. The villagers had celebrated his victory, but Vritra knew that the real battle was not just with rakshasas but with the very nature of trust and betrayal.

He replayed the events of the day in his mind, trying to understand how he had been so easily deceived. Sudhir had seemed so genuine, so eager to help. Vritra had seen no reason to doubt him, yet that very trust had almost led to his defeat. The thought that someone could so easily exploit his vulnerabilities filled him with a deep sense of unease.

As he stared into the flowing river, Vritra's mind wandered back to his training with his guru. His teacher had often spoken of the dangers that were not just physical but also emotional and psychological. "A warrior's greatest challenge," his guru had said, "is to see beyond the surface, to understand that not all enemies come with weapons drawn. Some strike from the shadows, using your own heart against you."

Vritra had always understood these lessons in theory, but now he realized the true depth of their meaning. The battle with Sudhir had been more than just a test of strength—it had been a test of Vritra's wisdom, his ability to discern friend from foe. He had failed that test, and it had nearly cost him everything.

Suddenly, a voice interrupted his thoughts. "You look troubled, Vritra."

Vritra turned to see his guru standing behind him, his wise eyes full of understanding. The old man had appeared as if out of nowhere, a habit of his that Vritra had never quite understood.

"Guruji," Vritra said, bowing his head in respect. "I was deceived today. I trusted someone who sought to destroy me. How could I have been so blind?"

The guru sat down beside Vritra, looking out over the river. "Deception is a powerful weapon," he said calmly. "It preys on the best parts of us—our kindness, our willingness to see the good in others. But do not be too harsh on yourself, Vritra. Trust is not a weakness. It is what makes you human, what connects you to others.

The challenge is not to stop trusting, but to be wise in whom you trust."

Vritra nodded, though his heart still felt heavy. "But how can I protect myself from being deceived again?"

The guru placed a hand on Vritra's shoulder. "By learning from this experience. By honing not just your physical strength, but your intuition, your ability to see beyond the surface. The world is full of shadows, Vritra, and not all of them are cast by the light. You must learn to see what lies hidden within those shadows."

Vritra thought about this for a long moment. He realized that his guru was right. The battle with Sudhir had not been a failure, but a lesson. He had survived, and in doing so, he had gained a deeper understanding of the complexities of trust and deception. This knowledge would make him a stronger warrior, one who could protect not just himself but the people he had sworn to defend.

His guru stood up, looking down at Vritra with a small smile. "Remember, Vritra, even the strongest warrior can be deceived. But it is how you recover, how you learn, that defines your strength. Do not let this experience harden your heart. Let it sharpen your mind."

With those words, the guru turned and walked away, leaving Vritra alone once more. But this time, Vritra felt a sense of clarity. He knew that his journey was far from over, and that there would be more challenges ahead— some of them more subtle and insidious than a rakshasa's physical attack.

As he rose to his feet, Vritra made a vow to himself. He would continue to protect the village, to fight against the forces of darkness. But he would also be more cautious, more discerning in whom he placed his trust. He would not let another Sudhir catch him off guard.

The moon was high in the sky by the time Vritra returned to the village. The streets were quiet, the people finally at peace after the day's turmoil. Vritra walked through the silent lanes, feeling the weight of his responsibilities more acutely than ever before. He had learned a valuable lesson, one that would guide him in the battles to come.

But as he reached his home, a thought lingered at the back of his mind—a question that he couldn't quite shake. Had Sudhir been acting alone, or was there a greater force at play? The rakshasa he had defeated had been cunning and resourceful, but was it the true mastermind, or just a pawn in a larger game?

Vritra knew that his journey was far from over. The shadows that had brought Sudhir into his life were still out there, lurking just beyond his sight. And though he had won this battle, the war against the darkness was only just beginning.

As he lay down to rest, Vritra's thoughts were not of victory, but of preparation. He would need to be ready for whatever came next. The enemy was clever, and it would not stop until it had found a way to defeat him. But Vritra was no longer the same warrior he had been before. He had faced betrayal and had come out stronger for it.

The battle against the hidden enemy was far from over, and Vritra was determined to be ready for whatever came next. The night was dark, but Vritra knew that dawn would come—and with it, a new day of challenges and victories. He would face them all, for he was Vritra, the warrior destined to protect his people, no matter the cost.

Chapter 6: *The Conflict of Love and Duty*

Vritra returned to the village, his heart still racing from the battle against the rakshasas. The key to the ancient manuscript was a tangible reminder of the immense power he wielded, but as he stepped through the familiar paths of his home, he felt a different kind of energy stirring within him—a desire for connection that transcended the battles he fought.

It was on one such day, while he was helping to rebuild a house damaged during the chaos, that he met Anushka. She was a vision of grace, her laughter ringing like music in the air, her eyes sparkling with intelligence and compassion. Vritra found himself drawn to her, captivated not just by her beauty, but by her unwavering spirit as she tended to the needs of the villagers.

"Thank you for helping," Anushka said, her voice gentle yet firm as she handed him a wooden beam. "You fought bravely for us. The village is lucky to have you."

"I'm just doing what needs to be done," Vritra replied, feeling a warmth spread through him at her acknowledgment. "I can't let evil threaten my home."

As days turned into weeks, Vritra and Anushka's bond deepened. They spent countless hours together, sharing stories and laughter amidst the backdrop of the village. She was not only his anchor in a world filled with chaos but also a confidante who listened as he shared tales of his battles and the burdens he carried.

But beneath the surface of their growing affection lay a storm. The darkness was relentless, and each confrontation with the rakshasas drained him, drawing him further away from the normalcy Anushka craved. The village remained tense, the threat of the monstrous forces ever-present, and with every victory came the lingering shadow of defeat.

One evening, as they sat beneath the sprawling branches of an ancient banyan tree, Anushka took a deep breath, her brow furrowed with worry. "Vritra, I know your heart is noble, but what of your own happiness? You fight for the village, for everyone, but what about you? What do you want?"

Vritra's heart raced as he met her gaze. "I want to protect you, Anushka. I want to ensure this village is safe. That is my duty."

"But at what cost?" she pressed, her voice trembling with emotion. "You could leave this all behind. We could find a peaceful life together, away from the darkness. You don't have to carry this burden alone."

Vritra felt a pang in his chest. The thought of a life filled with love and peace was alluring, but the weight of his responsibility anchored him. "I cannot abandon my mission. The raptors are growing stronger, and they will not rest until they claim this land. If I don't fight, who will?"

Anushka's eyes glistened with unshed tears. "And if you lose yourself in this fight? What will become of us? What will become of you?"

The conflict within Vritra surged like a tempest. The pull of his duty warred against the burgeoning love he felt for Anushka. As days passed, he found himself increasingly torn, caught in the crossfire of duty and desire.

That night, as he lay awake under the stars, he recalled his mentor's teachings: "A guardian must balance strength with compassion. Power alone is not enough; the heart must guide the hand." The words echoed in his mind, intensifying his internal struggle.

Vritra resolved to confront the growing darkness, hoping that by vanquishing the rakshasas once and for all, he could return to a life free of fear and be with Anushka. With newfound determination, he gathered the villagers and strategized their next move against the rakshasaic threat.

But as he prepared, a shadow lurked on the periphery—Sudhir, the covert enemy he had defeated, had left behind more than just remnants of his dark power. Whispers of a more sinister plot began to surface, leading Vritra to suspect that the rakshasas were organizing under a single, formidable leader.

"Tonight, we strike," Vritra announced one afternoon, standing before the gathered villagers. "We will confront the rakshasas and put an end to their reign of terror once and for all."

Anushka stepped forward, a mixture of fear and defiance in her eyes. "Vritra, please, think this through. You cannot do this alone! You need to consider your safety and ours."

"Anushka, this is our chance to reclaim our home," he replied, desperation creeping into his voice. "I must protect you, protect everyone. I cannot let fear dictate our lives any longer."

But beneath her fear lay something deeper—an unwavering belief in his power. "You're stronger than you realize, but even the strongest need support. You don't have to face this alone."

The tension crackled between them, a storm brewing on the horizon. Vritra sensed that the moment of confrontation was drawing near. As they prepared for battle, he could feel Anushka's gaze upon him, filled with both trust and worry.

That night, as the villagers gathered around the fire to share tales of bravery and courage, Vritra's mind was elsewhere. He felt a burning desire to protect Anushka and the village, but the thought of losing her haunted him.

Suddenly, a low growl reverberated through the air, drawing everyone's attention. From the darkness emerged a massive figure cloaked in shadow—the rakshasa leader, Kaalasura. Its eyes glowed with malice, scanning the crowd.

"Foolish mortals," the rakshasa taunted, its voice dripping with contempt. "You think you can defeat me? Your guardian is but a flickering candle in the abyss of darkness!"

Vritra stepped, heart racing but resolute. "I am no mere candle; I am Vritra, protector of this land. I will not let you destroy what we have fought so hard to defend!"

The Kaalasura chuckled, a sound filled with malice. "Ah, Vritra, the hero. How amusing. But your courage is futile. You cannot win against the shadows that thrive on your fears."

As Vritra faced the rakshasa, he felt Anushka's presence beside him, grounding him with her unwavering support. "Together," she whispered, squeezing his hand tightly. "You're not alone in this."

The villagers, emboldened by Vritra's determination, formed a circle around him. They held torches and weapons, ready to fight for their lives and their home. The firelight danced, illuminating their fierce expressions of resolve against the encroaching darkness.

With a roar, Kaalasura lunged forward, claws outstretched. Vritra raised his Vajra, channeling the ancient power within him, the energy thrumming through his body as he summoned the strength of the earth and sky. He unleashed a barrage of bolts, lightning cascading from the sky, striking the rakshasa with blinding force.

But Kaalasura was not easily defeated. It twisted through the air, dodging the attacks and retaliating with blasts of dark energy that sent villagers tumbling. Panic spread, and Vritra could feel the shadows closing in on their hopes.

"Stay focused! We fight together!" he shouted, rallying his people. He unleashed wave after wave of powerful strikes, each hit a testament to his determination, yet Kaalasura absorbed the energy, growing more powerful with each blow.

Anushka, filled with an indomitable spirit, stepped forward. "Vritra! Remember the manuscript! It spoke of harnessing our combined energies!"

"Combined energies?" Vritra echoed, a flicker of realization igniting within him. "Yes! The strength of our unity!"

Vritra turned to the villagers. "We need to channel our strength together! Focus your energy on me, on our fight! We can weaken it together!"

As they aligned their thoughts and energies, a radiant light enveloped Vritra, growing brighter with every chant and incantation uttered by the villagers. Anushka stood by his side, her eyes shining with determination, her heart beating in sync with his.

Kaalasura staggered, momentarily thrown off by the brilliant light. "What is this sorcery?" it hissed, rage boiling in its voice.

"This is the power of unity, of love and duty intertwined!" Vritra declared, feeling an electric surge. "We stand as one!"

With that, they unleashed their combined energy in a blinding beam, illuminating the night and piercing through the darkness that surrounded them. Kaalasura screeched, flailing in an attempt to shield itself, but the radiant light consumed it, dissolving its shadowy form into nothingness.

As the glow subsided, silence fell over the battlefield. The villagers stared in awe, their hearts pounding with adrenaline and relief. Vritra, though exhausted, felt a profound sense of triumph swell within him. They had done it—they had faced the darkness and emerged victorious.

But as he turned to Anushka, he saw a shadow pass over her face. "Anushka?" he asked, concern creeping into his voice. "What's wrong?"

"I felt something..." she began, her voice trembling. "When we fought Kaalasura, there was a presence, something even darker lurking just beyond. I think... I think this isn't over."

Vritra's heart sank. He had hoped that this victory would mean safety, but Anushka's intuition was rarely wrong. "We must remain vigilant," he replied, determination igniting within him once more. "If there are more threats out there, we will face them together."

Days passed, and the village slowly began to rebuild, the remnants of fear dissipating with each act of kindness and courage shared among the villagers. Yet, the unease lingered, a quiet whisper that echoed through Vritra's mind.

He sought out his mentor, the wise priest who had guided him through his trials. "Guruji," Vritra said, bowing respectfully, "I sense a greater darkness still lurks. What must I do to prepare for the challenges ahead?"

The priest looked at him, his eyes heavy with ancient wisdom. "The path of a protector is fraught with challenges, Vritra. You have faced rakshasas, but remember, true strength lies not only in power but in understanding the heart of darkness. You must seek knowledge beyond what you have, delve into the secrets of the ancient manuscripts. Only then can you anticipate and counter what lies in wait."

Vritra nodded, the weight of his responsibilities pressing down on him. "I will seek the knowledge needed to protect my home and Anushka."

With renewed resolve, Vritra decided to continue the search for the ancient key, the one that would unlock the manuscript containing secrets of immense power. He gathered a group of trusted villagers, and they ventured into the depths of the forest where rumors spoke of the key hidden within an ancient temple.

As they navigated the treacherous paths, the air thickened with tension. The forest whispered secrets, and shadows danced just beyond the light of their torches. Vritra could feel a presence watching them, a sense of being followed by something unseen.

Suddenly, a chilling laugh echoed through the trees. "You think you can find the key? Foolish mortals!" The voice was unmistakably sinister, dripping with malice.

From the shadows emerged a figure draped in darkness, its form shifting like smoke. "I am the keeper of the key, and you will pay for your arrogance."

"Show yourself!" Vritra demanded, brandishing his Vajra. "We are not afraid of you!"

The figure laughed again, a sound that sent shivers down their spines. "You will be. You have no idea what horrors await you. The darkness has only begun to awaken."

Before Vritra could respond, the figure lunged forward, and chaos erupted. Shadows swirled around them, pulling at their energy and sapping their strength. Vritra fought back, summoning the light of his Vajra, but the darkness was relentless, trying to engulf them.

"Stay close!" he shouted, trying to keep his companions together. Anushka stood resolute at his side, determination gleaming in her eyes.

Together, they fought against the onslaught of shadows, their unity igniting sparks of light that pushed back against the darkness. But it was clear they were outmatched. The shadowy figure twisted and turned, slipping through their defenses, striking from the edges of their vision.

Vritra knew they had to reach the heart of the darkness to banish it once and for all. "We need to find the temple! The key must be close!" he urged, forcing his way through the chaos toward the flickering glow of the ancient structure.

As they neared the temple, the shadows intensified, clawing at their resolve. Vritra and Anushka pushed forward, hand in hand, their hearts beating as one. "Together," she whispered, her voice barely audible above the cacophony.

With one final push, they burst into the temple, the air charged with ancient energy. Inside, they found a pedestal bathed in ethereal light, atop which lay a magnificent key, glimmering with promise.

But as Vritra reached for it, the shadowy figure materialized in the doorway, its form coalescing into something monstrous, a grotesque mockery of the protector he aspired to be. "You will not take it! The key belongs to me!" it roared, unleashing a wave of darkness that threatened to consume everything.

With a roar of defiance, Vritra lifted his Vajra, the light flaring brighter than ever before. "You will not claim this world! I fight for all that is good and just!"

The key pulsed with energy, resonating with Vritra's resolve. He turned to Anushka, who nodded, her eyes fierce with conviction. "Now, Vritra!"

Together, they summoned all their strength, channeling their love and unity into a blinding burst of light. The shadows recoiled, their hold on the temple breaking as the radiance enveloped everything.

With a final surge of energy, Vritra reached for the key, grasping it tightly. The moment he touched it, a shockwave erupted, sending the shadowy figure spiraling back, its form disintegrating into wisps of smoke.

The temple is filled with blinding light, illuminating the ancient symbols carved into its walls. Vritra felt the power of the manuscript surge within him, unlocking the secrets of strength and wisdom he needed to combat the darkness.

As the last remnants of the shadow faded, Vritra turned to Anushka, their eyes meeting with a shared understanding. They had faced the darkness together and emerged victorious, but the battle was far from over. With the key in hand, they held the promise of knowledge and strength, ready to confront whatever lay ahead.

Together, they stepped out of the temple, knowing that love and duty would guide them as they prepared to face the true force of darkness that awaited them. The journey was far from over, but they were no longer alone in their fight. They had each other, and together, they would light the way through the shadows.

Chapter 7: *The Revelation of Powers*

With the ancient key now in his possession, Vritra stood at the threshold of ultimate power. The air crackled with energy as he poured over the ancient manuscript, uncovering secrets that had lain dormant for centuries. He learned that his abilities, while formidable, were not yet fully awakened. The manuscript detailed a sacred ritual designed to unleash his full potential, a process that promised to elevate him to unimaginable heights.

However, the path to enlightenment was fraught with danger. The ritual required him to become vulnerable, exposing him to the very forces he sought to conquer. Vritra confided in Anushka and his mentor, the wise guru who had guided him through countless trials. Concern etched across their faces; they urged caution. "This is a dangerous path, Vritra," his guru warned. "You must be prepared for what may come."

Ignoring their warnings would mean putting them at risk, but Vritra felt an insatiable drive within him. He knew that without this power, he could never hope to protect the ones he loved. After a night filled with restless thoughts, he made his decision.

As dawn broke, Vritra began the ritual in a secluded grove, far from the village. Anushka stood by his side, her hands trembling as she gripped his. "Promise me you'll be careful," she whispered, her voice barely audible over the rustling leaves.

"I promise," he replied, though doubt gnawed at him.

He placed the ancient key atop a stone altar, a focal point for the energies he was about to summon. The sunbathed the grove in a golden light, and Vritra closed his eyes, drawing upon the essence of nature, the power of the earth, and the strength of his ancestors.

But just as the energy began to swell, a chilling wind swept through the grove, and shadows emerged from the treeline. The rakshasas had come to thwart him, their eyes glowing with malevolence. They surged forward, howling in delight at the opportunity to destroy their greatest foe.

"Anushka! Stay back!" Vritra shouted, summoning the first wave of his powers. Lightning crackled around him as he channeled energy into a barrier, protecting Anushka while trying to focus on the ritual.

The rakshasas, undeterred, flung themselves against his shield. Anushka fought valiantly, her determination burning bright as she wielded a staff imbued with the essence of the forest. Vritra could see her efforts straining against the onslaught, and his heart ached with the weight of his choice.

"Focus, Vritra! You must complete the ritual!" she cried, fending off the advancing shadows. The rakshasas were relentless, clawing at the edges of his protective sphere, attempting to break through.

Summoning every ounce of strength, Vritra drew upon the bond they shared, feeling Anushka's spirit intertwining with his own. He envisioned their love as a powerful force, one that could not be extinguished by darkness. The energy surged within him, growing more potent with each heartbeat.

As the shadows pressed in, Vritra felt a pulse of raw power igniting within him. "I am not afraid!" he shouted, and in that moment, he unleashed a torrent of energy that exploded outward.

The grove lit up with blinding light as he completed the ritual. A shockwave emanated from him, knocking the rakshasas back and shattering the darkness that clung to them. Vritra's form transformed, a brilliant aura encasing him, illuminating the entire grove. He felt the awakening of every dormant part of himself, the very essence of power flowing through his veins.

But the rakshasas were not finished. "You may have gained strength, but it will not save you!" their leader snarled, reforming from the shadows. "We will consume you, Vritra, and take your power for ourselves!"

In the face of this threat, Vritra stood firm. With Anushka at his side, they prepared for the battle of their lives. Together, they launched themselves into the fray, a whirlwind of light and shadow. The grove became a battleground, the air filled with the crackling energy of clashing forces.

Vritra fought with newfound ferocity, each strike imbued with the power of the earth, and each spell woven with the fabric of the universe. Anushka's strength fueled his resolve as they danced through the chaos, a harmonious blend of love and power that shook the very ground beneath them.

But just as they seemed to gain the upper hand, the leader of the rakshasas unleashed a sinister laugh, summoning reinforcements from the depths of darkness. Shadows twisted and coalesced into a swarm of monstrous forms, threatening to overwhelm them.

"Anushka!" Vritra shouted, fear coursing through him. "We need to find a way to turn their strength against them!"

"Follow my lead!" she replied, her eyes ablaze with determination. Together, they coordinated their attacks, targeting the leader with strategic precision, while fending off the lesser rakshasas that sought to drag them down.

The battle raged on, a clash of titans as light fought against the encroaching darkness. Vritra felt his energy waning, but the thought of losing Anushka spurred him onward. He couldn't allow the darkness to take her away.

Just when all hope seemed lost, the ancient key began to resonate with the energy of the battle. It pulsed with life, and Vritra realized that it was not just a tool, but a conduit for the collective strength of the earth, the people, and their love.

"Anushka! The key! We need to use it!" he yelled, his voice rising above the chaos.

As she grasped the key tightly, Vritra felt a connection form between them, a bond that transcended the physical realm. They poured their energy into the key, their love illuminating the darkness around them.

With a brilliant flash, the key transformed into a radiant weapon of light, and Vritra raised it high. "This ends now!" he declared, channeling their combined strength into a single, powerful strike.

The energy surged forth, piercing through the heart of the darkness and exploding outward in a shockwave that shattered the rakshasas' ranks. The leader screeched, its form unraveling as the light consumed it. One by one, the remaining rakshasas were cast into oblivion, their shadows dissipating into the ether.

As silence fell over the grove, Vritra and Anushka stood together, panting from the exertion of battle. They had emerged victorious, but the cost weighed heavily on them.

"We did it," Anushka breathed, her eyes shining with tears of relief.

"Yes," Vritra replied, but doubt lingered in his heart. "But I fear this is only the beginning."

Chapter 8: *The Preparation for the Final War*

In the aftermath of their victory, Vritra's senses sharpened. Despite their triumph over the rakshasas, whispers of a greater evil grew louder in his mind. The darkness had retreated, but its power still loomed on the horizon, an ominous shadow threatening to engulf their world once again.

"We cannot rest," he said to Anushka and his mentor. "There's a new threat brewing, and we must prepare for what lies ahead."

His guru nodded gravely. "The battles we face will not only test your strength but also your resolve. We must gather allies, forge new bonds, and prepare for the challenges yet to come."

As they set to work, Vritra summoned trusted allies from nearby villages—warriors, mages, and wise sages who had heard tales of his bravery. With each addition to their ranks, their confidence grew. Yet, in the depths of Vritra's heart, unease lingered like a storm cloud.

The nights grew darker, and the stars seemed to dim as an ancient malevolence awakened, plotting in the shadows. Vritra felt it creeping closer, a cold breath at his neck, whispering despair.

"Prepare the defenses! Train the villagers!" Vritra commanded, organizing drills and strategic meetings. "We must stand united!"

As days turned into weeks, the village transformed into a bastion of hope. Together, they forged weapons imbued with light, warding off the encroaching darkness. Vritra trained tirelessly, honing his skills, while Anushka worked to strengthen the bonds among the villagers.

Yet, despite their efforts, the shadows gathered, and every day brought new reports of strange occurrences: crops failing, livestock disappearing, and eerie sounds echoing through the night. The very land seemed to be poisoned by an unseen force.

"We need to understand what we're up against," Vritra said, pacing before his assembled allies. "Our enemy grows stronger, and we must learn their weaknesses."

They decided to send scouts into the depths of the forest, seeking answers from the wise elders who lived in hidden enclaves. Legends spoke of ancient beings who possessed knowledge of the darkest magic, and Vritra believed they might hold the key to defeating the looming threat.

As they prepared for the expedition, Anushka approached him, concern shadowing her features. "What if you find something that changes everything? What if you discover that this darkness is more powerful than we can comprehend?"

Vritra grasped her hands, the warmth of her touch igniting his resolve. "No matter what we face, I will always return to you. Together, we will confront the darkness."

With their plan set, Vritra led a small group into the heart of the forest, the air thick with tension. As they traversed the twisted paths, the trees seemed to close in around them, shadows creeping along the ground.

Deep in the forest, they encountered the elders, ancient beings whose wisdom stretched across millennia. They spoke in riddles, their voices like rustling leaves.

"You seek to understand the darkness," one elder said, eyes gleaming like embers. "But know this: it feeds on fear and doubt. It grows stronger in the shadows of uncertainty."

Vritra listened intently, absorbing their teachings. "What can we do to combat it?"

"The key lies within you," another elder replied. "But to unlock it, you must confront your own fears and embrace the light within."

Returning to the village, Vritra felt a shift within himself, a realization that the true battle was not just against the external darkness, but also within his own heart. The villagers looked to him for hope, and he knew he could not falter.

As the final preparations for battle commenced, a sudden chill filled the air. An ominous darkness enveloped the village, and from it emerged the silhouette of a massive figure.

Vritra's heart sank as he recognized the rakshasa leader, somehow restored and more powerful than before. "You think you can prepare for war?" it boomed, voice echoing like thunder. "I will destroy everything you love!"

The villagers gasped, fear flooding their hearts, but Vritra stood firm. "You will not win! We are united, and we will stand against you!"

The rakshasa laughed, a cruel sound that reverberated through the village. "You think your unity can save you? The true darkness is yet to come. Prepare for your end!"

With that, it vanished back into the shadows, leaving behind a chilling sense of dread. Vritra knew that the final war was upon them, and this time, the stakes were higher than ever.

Chapter 9: *The Final Stand*

The day of reckoning dawned, and a heavy cloud loomed over the village. Vritra stood atop the hill, looking out at the gathering storm. He could sense the darkness closing in, an impending wave of despair that threatened to swallow them whole.

"Today, we fight!" he declared to the assembled villagers and allies. "We will not cower in the face of fear; we will stand united and push back against the shadows!"

The warriors cheered, but Vritra could see the flickers of doubt in their eyes. He stepped down, speaking to his allies one by one, instilling courage and hope in their hearts. Anushka stood at his side, her presence a beacon of light in the growing darkness.

As the sun dipped below the horizon, the first wave of shadows descended upon them, monstrous shapes coalescing into form. The air thickened with the smell of fear, and Vritra felt it tightening around him.

"Remember our training! Hold the line!" he shouted, raising his Vajra as the first rakshasa charged. The battle erupted, a clash of light and dark as warriors fought valiantly, driven by the hope of a brighter tomorrow.

Vritra fought alongside Anushka, their movements synchronized, each strike a testament to their bond. The villagers rallied around them, a united front against the encroaching darkness.

But the rakshasa leader appeared once more, its form shifting and twisting in the chaos. "You think you can defeat me?" it roared, charging toward them with an army of shadows. "This world belongs to me!"

Vritra felt the weight of its words, the very essence of fear attempting to seep into his heart. He shook his head, casting the doubt aside. "We are not alone! We stand together!"

With renewed resolve, he unleashed a powerful surge of energy, the Vajra glowing brightly as he called upon the strength of the earth, the spirits of his ancestors, and the love that bound him to Anushka. The light pushed back against the encroaching shadows, creating a barrier of hope.

But as they fought, the rakshasa leader absorbed the chaos around it, growing stronger with each passing moment. Vritra realized that they were running out of time. "We need to find a way to weaken it! Anushka, what did the elders say about confronting fear?"

"Embrace it," she replied, her voice steady even in the midst of chaos. "We must face it head-on."

With that revelation, Vritra stepped forward, facing the rakshasa leader as it towered above him. "You may be powerful, but you will never extinguish the light of hope!" he shouted, channeling every ounce of his fear into a single, focused attack.

The rakshasa hesitated, confusion flickering across its monstrous features. Seizing the moment, Vritra unleashed a blinding wave of energy, the Vajra illuminating the night as it surged toward the darkness.

In that instant, he saw the flickers of uncertainty in the rakshasa's eyes, felt its power wavering. It roared in defiance, but the light engulfed it, dissolving the shadows and illuminating the battlefield with brilliant light.

As the chaos subsided, Vritra collapsed to his knees, panting heavily. Anushka rushed to his side, her eyes filled with pride and concern. "You did it, Vritra! You faced the darkness!"

But as the villagers began to celebrate their hard-won victory, a rumble echoed through the ground. The darkness was not yet vanquished; it had merely retreated, gathering strength for another assault. Vritra could feel it, a pulse of malevolence in the air.

"What have we awakened?" he muttered, dread settling in his heart.

Just then, the ground split open, and from it emerged a colossal shadow, dark and swirling, an entity of pure malevolence. Vritra's heart sank as he realized the true nature of their battle.

"This is only the beginning!" the entity boomed, its voice reverberating through the very fabric of the world. "I am the darkness that binds all fear, all despair. You cannot defeat me!"

Vritra exchanged a glance with Anushka, their connection stronger than ever. "We must find a way to stop it," he said, determination shining in his eyes.

As they prepared for the next confrontation, Vritra's mind raced. The key, the manuscript, the ancient wisdom—they all pointed to something greater. But would it be enough to face this new threat?

With the shadows closing in once more, Vritra turned to the gathered allies, resolve igniting in his chest. "We may face an enemy we cannot see, but together we will confront it! We will fight until our last breath, for the light must never fade!"

But in the depths of his heart, a question lingered, an unsettling thought that gnawed at him: **Would they truly be able to defeat this darkness, or was it merely the first chapter of an even greater saga yet to unfold?**

To Be Continued...

As the battle loomed on the horizon, Vritra and Anushka prepared for the war ahead, aware that their journey was far from over. The fate of their world hung in the balance, and with each passing moment, the darkness awaited its chance to strike again. What awaited them in the shadows? What secrets would be revealed? The true battle had just begun...